Samuel French Acting Edition

Amelia

by Alex Webb

FOR PRODUCTION ENQUIRIES

UNITED STATES AND CANADA
Info@SamuelFrench.com
1-866-598-8449

UNITED KINGDOM AND EUROPE
Plays@SamuelFrench.co.uk
020-7255-4302

Each title is subject to availability from Samuel French, depending upon country of performance. Please be aware that *AMELIA* may not be licensed by Samuel French in your territory. Professional and amateur producers should contact the nearest Samuel French office or licensing partner to verify availability.

AMELIA premiered at the Washington Stage Guild in the Undercroft Theatre on January 5, 2012. The founding artistic director was John MacDonald. The production was produced by Ann Norton and directed by Bill Largess, with set design by Carl Gudenius and Kirk Kristlibas, lighting design by Marianne Meadows, costume design by Sigríður Jóhannesdóttir, sound design by Stowe Nelson, and wig design by Lynn Steinmetz. The stage manager was Arthur Nordlie and the assistant stage manager was Jessica Skelton, assisted by Andranik Kaladjian-Webb. The cast was as follows:

AMELIA . . . . Shirleyann Kaladjian
ETHAN & OTHERS . . . . .Alex Webb

CHARACTERS

AMELIA – Pennsylvania farmer

DADDY – Amelia's father

MAMA – Amelia's mother

BEN WYATT – a neighbor

ETHAN – Union soldier

MARIE – Amelia's former schoolmate

QUARTERMASTER – Union supply officer

SAWBONES – Union doctor at Gettysburg

CORPORAL HAWKINS – Union soldier at Gettysburg

HORSE THIEF – Confederate soldier

SAMUEL – escaped slave

DEAD EYES – Union soldier

VERMONT – Union corpse

COLONEL – severely wounded Union officer

MRS. SULLIVAN – destitute southern mother

COL. BINDER – Commander of Fort Wagner

BALTIMORE – Union soldier

DRIVER – Confederate soldier

KETCHAM – Andersonville prisoner, one arm

MORTON – raider at Andersonville

GUARD – guard at Andersonville

SETTING

1860s America, several locations

AUTHOR'S NOTES

Amelia was originally conceived and performed with two actors – one actress to play Amelia and one actor to play all other characters. There were no props and the set was minimal and abstract – a bench, a split-rail fence, a tree stump, and other simple structures that could stand in for the Quartermaster's front desk, Andersonville prisoner wagon, Mama's kitchen, etc.

Amelia had great success when it was able to move in this very fluid style. The audience is really the third actor and it is their imagination, aided by the seamless flow and pace of the show, that carries the day. Anything that slows that forward momentum of story or interrupts the audience's imagination/participation – a shift to a new set, for example – is death.

I have laid out a breakdown of how characters could be distributed in a five-actor professional version, for companies that want or require a larger cast:

AMELIA. . . . . Woman 1

MAMA, MARIE, MRS. SULLIVAN. . . . . Woman 2

ETHAN, DADDY, CORP. HAWKINS, COLONEL, BALTIMORE . . . . . Man 1

BEN WYATT, QUARTERMASTER, SAWBONES, MORTON
      GUARD, KETCHAM, HORSE THIEF . . . . Man 2

SAMUEL, COL. BINDER, DRIVER, VERMONT, DEAD EYES . . . . Man 3

Finally, for school/non-professional productions, I am comfortable with any casting breakdown that allows for as many to participate as desired. I am also willing to consider (in amateur productions) substitutions in the few cases where the language would be inappropriate for younger audiences.

For Shirleyann

AMELIA. First thing Daddy would tell people, after showing 'em his black and purple scar running foot to kneecap – first thing he'd say, pointing over at me: "See that gal right there, little slip of a thing. Stared down a two thousand pound Brahma bull. My lil' baby there – that girl is fearless."

I always loved that story. Half-true of course. Sure – I didn't flinch. I was thrilled. Standing there in the high grass staring down that beast. But…I was six years old. I was fearless alright…but only because I had no idea what that bull could do.

Mama understood. She knew exactly what she was up against. She'd just seen that bull hook one of Daddy's legs good and send him flying. Even so…she hurdled that fence without a thought and parked herself right in front of me.

Mama must've locked eyes with that bull for an hour. Finally that old devil decides it just ain't worth all the aggravation. And just like that with one last snort he saunters off to eat some grass like nothing ever happened.

Mama shaking all over. She drags Daddy out of the pasture, yelling at me to run ahead – never once taking her eyes off that bull. We get to the other side of the fence. Finally Mama can see everyone's safe – she just drops onto all fours weeping, howling like I never seen her before or since.

At the time, I didn't really understand just how much Mama had to lose in that moment…and just how brave that made her.

Coming in here looking for you – I guess it's like Mama. Scared out my mind. Knowing full well what's in front of me – but my feet kept moving anyway, one in front of the other, through that giant gate.

    (A shuddering slam, and a blackout, interrupted by:)

DADDY. *(Offstage.)* Amelia!

AMELIA. Over here, Daddy.

    *(**DADDY** enters, limping.)*

DADDY. Hey, girl.

AMELIA. Hey.

DADDY. You finished up at the dairy?

AMELIA. Yes, sir.

DADDY. Mama wants your help with dinner.

AMELIA. Yes sir.

    *(**AMELIA** tries to exit.)*

DADDY. Don't you want to know why?

AMELIA. No sir.

    (Tries again.)

DADDY. We've got a guest coming!

AMELIA. That's nice.

    (Tries once more.)

DADDY. Don't you want to know who?

AMELIA. I'm sure I'll find out…

DADDY. I just figured you'd be interested…

AMELIA. Daddy!

DADDY. Ben Wyatt's coming over from the mill. Seems like a nice fella and well we got to talking…

AMELIA. Daddy you didn't. Oh lord. Mama!!

DADDY. *(Nods to himself.)* That seemed to go well.

AMELIA. *(Runs into kitchen.)* Mama! How could you?!

MAMA. *(Working a mixing bowl.)* Listen to me Amelia, before you go flying off, let me just explain something to you! The secret to your father and I lasting as long as we have is well, we don't talk.

(Shouting toward **DADDY**.*)*

In other words the first I heard of Ben Wyatt coming over was – two minutes before you. Your daddy, I swear – well I don't swear but I can just imagine how good it would feel if I did.

AMELIA. He's coming up to the gate!

MAMA. Well, help me with these dumplings!

(Starts to leave, returns.)

Ohhh, I need more flour!

*(***MAMA*** exits.)*

DADDY. *(Offstage.)* *(Shouting.)* BEN! YOU CAN SET YOUR HORSE TO GRAZE OR JUST HITCH HIM UP OVER HERE.

*(***AMELIA*** brushes the dirt off the front of her dress as* **BEN WYATT** *enters, cock o' the walk.)*

AMELIA. Oh, excuse me, Mr. Wyatt. My daddy just told me you were here a few seconds ago.

(Shakes his hand.)

How are you?

BEN. Fine.

AMELIA. Well that's good to hear.

(Silence.)

How's everything at the mill?

BEN. Fine.

AMELIA. That's fine.

(Silence.)

AMELIA. Your horse?

BEN. Fine.

> *(Pause.)*

AMELIA. I heard the Redfields paid a lot for that new bull. Is he worth it?

BEN. Nope.

AMELIA. How's the corn up by you?

BEN. Fine.

AMELIA. I shoulda seen that comin'.

> *(Long pause.)*

Did you hear about Mr. Lincoln's speech against secession?

> *(Silence.)*

Mr. Wyatt?

BEN. Don't usually talk politics with ladies, ma'am.

AMELIA. *(Pause.)* Well, how about now?

BEN. *(Pause.)* Ma'am?

AMELIA. You say you don't usually talk politics with ladies and I'm asking how about now?

BEN. Could I see that mare?

AMELIA. Excuse me?

BEN. Your pa said he might have a mare to sell me.

AMELIA. Oh, that's how he...sure. Come on.

> *(They look over the horse.)*

There she is. The red chestnut. Maggie. She's got a good nature. Mr. Wyatt what would you be using her for at the mill?

BEN. Threshing.

AMELIA. *(Pats the horse.)* Threshing is mighty tedious work.

> *(Pause.)*

What do you do up to the mill?

BEN. Threshing.

(Pause.)

AMELIA. I guess we should be getting back to the house.

BEN. I'll be on my way.

AMELIA. Well you're still invited to dinner. I promise no politics.

BEN. Good evenin' then. Got a lot of chores to do with the daylight that's left.

AMELIA. Didn't you want to talk to Daddy about the mare?

(Pause.)

Well?

BEN. Nah, too much spirit for threshing work.

AMELIA. Her spirit's the best thing about her.

BEN. Well…not much daylight left, so…

AMELIA. Go ahead, you're so afraid of the dark.

(**BEN** *takes off,* **AMELIA** *wheels to face* **MAMA.**)

Where's Daddy?!

MAMA. *(Snapping green beans.)* Hidin'.

AMELIA. What could he be thinkin'? Ben Wyatt?

MAMA. I asked him the same thing.

AMELIA. What'd he say?

MAMA. "Forthright."

AMELIA. What does that mean?

MAMA. Amelia it has been thirty years and I still cannot extract any meaning from your father's one word answers. Does it to keep me interested.

AMELIA. AAAHHH! Ben Wyatt? The thing is…what does that say about Daddy's opinion of me?

MAMA. Oh, it don't say anything, honey, he's a man.

AMELIA. So?

MAMA. Men don't think normal. Don't get me wrong – you know I love your daddy forever – but sometimes they just have these wide, dull thoughts like: a woman as grown as Amelia ought to have a man. Makes no difference to him, which man. They just get up a "big plan" and proceed with a staggering vigor.

AMELIA. But even still Mama, Ben Wyatt? Do you know the main thing Ben likes to talk about?

(**MAMA** *shakes her head.*)

Threshing.

MAMA. Well, now, that's probably what your daddy likes about him. They can probably talk the finer points of threshing for hours.

AMELIA. I just don't get it.

MAMA. Well there's not much to it really you're just separating the wheat from the chaff and then…

AMELIA. No, Mama. This brazen need everyone has to pair up.

MAMA. Well, Amelia, honey, every woman's gotta find a husband.

AMELIA. Why? If I paired up with Ben I'd be more miserable than if I never lived.

MAMA. Oh Amelia, there's more to choose from than just Ben Wyatt.

AMELIA. A couple of widowers and a half-wit?

MAMA. There's a whole world of men out there…

AMELIA. And not a single one of them is interested in me or what I might have to say.

MAMA. We have talked about this before. A woman's job is to listen.

AMELIA. Well, I don't want that job, Mama. I got plenty o' work to do already.

MAMA. Well baby, a marriage…is more than that. It ain't just work.

AMELIA. Not from what I seen.

(**AMELIA** *exits scene, moves into general store.*)

MAMA. *(Calling after.)* Amelia, a man and a woman… There must be some reason we've been doing it this way for so long.

ETHAN. Can I help you ma'am?

AMELIA. Oh. I was looking for Mr. Johnson.

ETHAN. You've found him.

AMELIA. But…

ETHAN. Name's Ethan. Mr. Johnson's cousin from over to Lancaster. Helping out for the summer.

AMELIA. Oh. Nice to meet you.

ETHAN. It's a pleasure. Miss…?

AMELIA. Oh, yes. I'm sorry. Watson.

ETHAN. Miss Watson. Nice to meet you.

(They shake hands a little too long and then break.)

Can I help you?

AMELIA. Amelia.

ETHAN. Amelia.

(Pause.)

Can I help you?

AMELIA. Sure.

ETHAN. *(Pause.)* How?

AMELIA. Yes.

(Pulls herself together.) Two of the hundred-pounders of sweet feed, one barrel of flour, a keg of lard. Ten pounds of sugar. Not the Cuba sugar mind you, at that price. And two pouches of the Blackwell's tobacco.

ETHAN. *(Writing.)* Two?

AMELIA. Yes, two.

(Pause.)

It's for my daddy.

ETHAN. I figured as much.

AMELIA. What are you trying to say?

ETHAN. That I reckon it's for your pa.

AMELIA. What if it's for me?

ETHAN. But I thought you just said it was for your pa.

AMELIA. It is.

ETHAN. That's what I thought you said.

AMELIA. Okay then.

ETHAN. Okay then.

(*Pause.*)

Will there be anything else?

AMELIA. No.

ETHAN. I'll go ahead and load that up. That your shay out front?

AMELIA. Shay? There ain't no shay out there. If you mean the wagon with the red chestnut mare. Then, yes.

(*Pause,* **ETHAN** *smiles at her.*)

What?

ETHAN. I guess there's a little bit o' kick to you.

AMELIA. I don't know what you might mean by that.

ETHAN. Just an observation.

AMELIA. I came for supplies; not to be observed.

ETHAN. Sometimes you get more than you paid for.

AMELIA. I haven't paid.

ETHAN. Good point. You want to settle up now or put it on your daddy's bill?

AMELIA. I run the dairy on our farm and I've got my own tab with Mr. Johnson.

ETHAN. Smart woman.

AMELIA. That another one of your "observations." That I'm "a woman too smart for her own good"? Well it wouldn't be the first time I've heard that one.

ETHAN. I like smart women.

AMELIA. Oh.

ETHAN. So, if that's it… I guess I'll load up that "wagon."

AMELIA. Thank you.

ETHAN. I'm glad we met. "Amelia"…it sounds like a song.

(**AMELIA** *stares off after* **ETHAN** *for a moment, a little stunned.*)

MARIE. Amelia Watson. It's been ages.

AMELIA. *(Wakes up.)* Hello, Marie.

MARIE. Well, I guess just about everyone has stopped by for a little look-see.

AMELIA. Excuse me?

MARIE. Darling it's me, Marie. You're not really going to stand there and pretend you don't know what I'm talking about?

AMELIA. I'm not pretending. What are you talking about?

MARIE. Why, Mr. Johnson's cousin of course!

AMELIA. Oh, him.

MARIE. Yes, him. Every available Miss in the county put on her finest and rushed over here. To see him. Including you, I see. You're obviously snooping –

AMELIA. You think I'm snooping?!

MARIE. Oh, Amelia, please it is so conspicuously transparent what you are doing here!

AMELIA. I am not here because of any –

MARIE. Did he ask you to the social?

AMELIA. You take that back about me snooping around here! I just came to pick up supplies.

MARIE. So, he didn't ask you to the social! Well isn't that interesting. That's pretty much everyone… I guess he must already have –

AMELIA. Marie! Did you hear me? I am not interested in parading around for anyone's cousin!

> *(Pause.)*

What social?

MARIE. So you were snooping!

AMELIA. Marie, listen to me. I was not snooping! Not by a jug full!

MARIE. Amelia!

AMELIA. *(Louder.)* Was not!

MARIE. Alright!

(*Pause.*)

MARIE. You know, looking at that dress you're wearing, I almost believe you.

AMELIA. What's wrong with my dress?

MARIE. Where should I begin? Anyway, I did think you were a bit "mature."

AMELIA. You saying I'm too old for him?

MARIE. Well, Amelia, after all…

AMELIA. If anyone's too old to get married it's him.

MARIE. Yes, but he's a man.

AMELIA. So?

MARIE. Well, anyway, I'm glad to know you're off the list.

AMELIA. What list?

MARIE. Oh, Amelia! Why the list of ladies competing for Ethan's attentions.

AMELIA. Marie, even if I were interested in that arrogant, old clerk, I wouldn't run around flirting with him at the general store!

MARIE. Oh, really? Well, just how do you think these things occur? I mean, in the actual world.

AMELIA. I don't know, but I'm not interested in "trapping" a man like he was wild game!

MARIE. (*Laughs.*) Oh, Amelia, a woman's only job in this world is to beguile. That's how we ended up running the world. Or didn't you ever hear the story of Adam and Eve?

AMELIA. As a matter of fact, I read that story, and I understood them having no clothes as a metaphor for seeing the whole person.

MARIE. (*Pause.*) I have nothing to say to that. You always were different. So you won't be at the social.

AMELIA. Why not?

MARIE. Well, because you just said – well, you know – all those blasphemous ideas about Adam and Eve…

AMELIA. That doesn't mean I can't enjoy a party.

MARIE. But why would you go…if you don't want a man?

AMELIA. I'm going…'cause I'm going…don't always have to be about a man…

MARIE. *(Pause.)* I have nothing to say to that.

AMELIA. That's fine. Just tell me when and where.

MARIE. First Saturday of next month at the Ferry Landing.

AMELIA. *(Breathless.)* Mama! I need to make a dress.

MAMA. What?

AMELIA. I need a dress.

MAMA. I heard you the first time. I just don't understand you.

AMELIA. Which part's got you stumped?

MAMA. The needing part…and then the dress part.

AMELIA. Mama I just need your help figuring out a pattern – I don't want any questions.

MAMA. Questions? Why would I have any questions? I'm just your mama. It's just the first and only time you've ever asked me to help you with a dress. All you ever talk to me about is the dairy and what you caught hunting with your daddy. I'm just your mama. Why would I have any questions?

AMELIA. MAMA!

   (Pause, and then it pours out of her.)

So there is a fella at the general store and it's probably nothing but I think I might need to find out and Marie says there's a social a week from now and that every girl in the county is after him and well he said he liked smart women and I never heard a man say that before and well you ought to at least find out if a person really means something like that, don't you think?

MAMA. Oh, honey!

AMELIA. Now, Mama. It's gonna turn out to be nothing. So let's not get all worked up. Just help me with the dress.

MAMA. *(Calm, taking* **AMELIA***'s cue.)* Oh-kay.

> *(Gradually getting worked up again and running off.)*

I know just the pattern! Eliza down the road showed it to me! Oh, you are just going to fall in love with it. ELIZA! HELLOOO! NOW WAIT'LL YOU HEAR THIS…

> *(***AMELIA*** watches* **MAMA** *go.)*

> *(The sounds of a party come up and* **AMELIA** *stands there – a classic wallflower.* **MARIE** *sees her from across the room and glides over.)*

MARIE. Amelia Watson that is a new dress, and you told me you were off the list!

AMELIA. A person can have a new dress without being on a list.

MARIE. You're back on the list! And after assuring me that you had no interest!

AMELIA. Will you stop talking about the list! There is no list. The only list is in your addled brain. "The list" is just a bunch of empty-headed girls with their ridiculous bows, awful shoes and stupid ribbons in their hair lookin' like a bunch of tarts!

> *(***MARIE*** gasps.)*

What could I have been thinking? Wasting an hour at this social has been the longest year of my life! "Social"! I'd like to know what's social about it – just a big room full of nerves and fake laughter.

MARIE. *(Stunned, then bursts out in fake laughter.)* Oh, Amelia you are so amusing!

AMELIA. What?

MARIE. He's here!

Ethan Johnson! Why Miss Watson was just telling me the funniest story. Oh, do tell him Amelia!

AMELIA. What are you talking about?

MARIE. Oh, you know!

AMELIA. Nope.

MARIE. Well, it was just so amusing and unexpected!

> *(Pause.)*

Surely you haven't forgotten after only just telling me?!

AMELIA. Yup.

MARIE. Well, Mr. Johnson, it was certainly amusing at the time.

Ethan, I must tell you what a trial it was to finally decide on this dress! I said to myself, "Marie I wish your pretty little head worked a little better!" I just could *not* remember, to save my life, what your favorite color was! Now did you tell me green or red?

AMELIA. Excuse me.

> **(AMELIA** *crosses the stage to leave the party.)*

ETHAN. Miss Watson!

> **(AMELIA** *keeps moving.)*

Miss Watson, I was hoping to speak with you!

> **(AMELIA** *keeps moving until* **ETHAN** *blocks her path.)*

Miss Watson, could you just wait a minute?

> **(AMELIA** *pushes past him.* **ETHAN** *blocks her again.)*

What are you so afraid of?

AMELIA. I ain't afraid of nothing!

ETHAN. Well…that's just stupid.

AMELIA. That does it!

> *(He reaches out, touches her arm.)*

ETHAN. Hold on, hold on! I'm sorry.

> *(Pause.)*

I just wanted to talk to you.

AMELIA. Looked to me like you were talking just fine with Marie.

ETHAN. Well that conversation pretty much flows in one direction.

AMELIA. Does it really?

ETHAN. Well, um, I guess I'd just rather talk to you.

AMELIA. Huh. I noticed that Marie seems to be pretty familiar with you.

ETHAN. She ought to – she comes by the store everyday.

AMELIA. Does she?

ETHAN. I tried explaining to her that if she wrote down a list of necessaries she might not have to stop by so much, you know, instead of just buying one little thing every day.

AMELIA. And what'd she say to that?

ETHAN. Not much. It seemed to stump her. Like when I asked her about Mr. Lincoln's speech.

AMELIA. *(Pause.)* Say that again.

ETHAN. I asked her about Mr. Lincoln's speech, you know, the one he just made against secession.

AMELIA. Mr. Johnson, are you saying that you would talk politics with a woman?

ETHAN. What's happening with secession right now – I'll talk about that with anyone, man, woman or child. It could change the way we live forever. And you know, I've been thinking… Ah, listen to me. I know what I think. What do you think?

AMELIA. *(Pause.)* Thank you for asking. I think Mr. Lincoln's words are some of the most powerful I've ever read… but what really scares me, Ethan, is that there seem to be an awful lot of ignorant people just spoiling for a fight.

ETHAN. I know, but how can we live with ourselves if we don't stand up and fight against something so flatout evil as slavery?

> *(Pause.)*

Hey, you called me Ethan.

AMELIA. That's your name, ain't it?

(Pause.)

I like that fiddler. You want to dance?

ETHAN. I don't really dance.

AMELIA. Neither do I.

(Pause.)

Which might make you wonder why I would ask you to dance. I don't really have an answer to that.

ETHAN. When I said I don't "really dance" that was probably optimistic on my part. If I dance with you right now that will make…exactly one time for me.

*(The music is slow and manageable. They look at each other for a long moment, and then **ETHAN** offers his arm. They move onto the dance floor. Just then, a new dance, much faster, is announced.)*

FIDDLER. *(Offstage.)* Devil's Stump, everyone!

*(They are jostled by the crowd. They watch the whirling circle of dancers. **ETHAN** starts clapping with no discernible rhythm. **AMELIA** stops him. She attempts to mimic the dancers' handholds with **ETHAN**. It's no good. They finally find the handhold and try to join in. Everything goes slowmo, they get spun around, and **ETHAN** falls down. **AMELIA** tries to help him up, he refuses, jumps up, and bravely attempts a horrible dance step. Back to normal speed – he goes on for a moment.)*

AMELIA. Ethan. Stop. Stop!

ETHAN. What's wrong with that?

(He keeps dancing.)

AMELIA. What's right with that?

ETHAN. You think you can do better?

AMELIA. A blind man could do better.

ETHAN. Well, why don't you lead then?

AMELIA. I think I will.

> (**AMELIA** *grabs* **ETHAN** *to show her idea of leading.*
> *Another terrible attempt ensues…and then she*
> *stops…*)

Ethan. Stop. Hold on.

ETHAN. Why? What's the matter.

> (*They both look around at the crowd.*)

AMELIA. Listen.

ETHAN. What? I don't hear anything.

AMELIA. Exactly. They stopped playing.

ETHAN. Oh my goodness. Where's the band? There was a band.

> (*Looks around.*)

You think our dancing scared 'em off?

> (*They both laugh.* **ETHAN** *announces:*)

No need to worry everyone. We're done for now! You can rest easy!

> (*They start to walk off.* **ETHAN** *moves back to*
> *center stage.*)

However, there will be another show in about thirty minutes! Come back then! It's free!

> (**ETHAN** *tries to bow, and* **AMELIA** *yanks him*
> *offstage.*)

> (**AMELIA** *re-appears downstage in a pool of light.*)

AMELIA. It's so unsettling when things are that good. You shook me.

Just took me in for good and liked every bit of it – and me for you.

A few weeks later – I'm hanging onto a dream by one thin spidery line when all of a sudden it snaps and I am yanked way, way up into that icy cold Pennsylvania morning with sweat running down my back… I could feel it coming.

*(Lights up on **DADDY** sitting, staring out a window in the house. **AMELIA** enters.)*

Morning, Daddy.

(Kisses him on the cheek and starts moving out the door.)

Shouldn't you already be out to the southwest corner? You said you were gonna tend to those cornfields.

DADDY. Yeah. I'll get to it. Had something to do here.

AMELIA. I've been trying that new milking and feed schedule from the German family east of town and ya know what? I'm getting about half again as much milk. I'm gonna make you a rich man!

DADDY. You always make me proud.

AMELIA. Hey! Where's Mama?

DADDY. Said she was feeling a little poorly, so she layed in.

AMELIA. What? Mama's sick?

*(**DADDY** looks down at the floor.)*

Daddy? What is it?

DADDY. I just want to apologize.

AMELIA. What could you have to apologize for?

DADDY. Ben Wyatt.

AMELIA. Ben Wyatt? Ben over at the mill? What's he got to do with anything?

DADDY. Sold you short.

AMELIA. Excuse me?

DADDY. You're everything a man could wish for in a daughter and here I am scrounging around for an old stiff like Ben Wyatt.

I guess I worried you were running out of time – when God knew all along – Ethan was coming, in his own time, and as fine a man as you'd ever hope to meet. And now… I'm just so sorry.

AMELIA. What are you saying?

*(**DADDY** tries to finish, can't, exits. **MAMA** enters.)*

Mama? Why is Daddy talkin' to me about Ben Wyatt?

MAMA. He ain't talking about Ben.

AMELIA. Well, what then?

MAMA. Fort Sumter's what he meant to say.

AMELIA. What?

MAMA. Beauregard just took over Fort Sumter. He's been firing on it for days. Your daddy just heard at the Post Office.

AMELIA. Mama?

MAMA. They been talkin' about it for a while. But…now they's done talkin'.

AMELIA. Are you sure?

MAMA. A war is gonna happen.

AMELIA. Daddy thinks Ethan will go and fight.

MAMA. Now, it doesn't have to be that way. Like I told your daddy –

AMELIA. Daddy is right to cry.

MAMA. Now, honey, you listen to me, listen –

AMELIA. Listen?! I never should have listened to you in the first place.

MAMA. What?

AMELIA. You said everyone's got to have someone… Well, I got someone, Mama, and now… I wish I never met him.

MAMA. Amelia!

> (**AMELIA** *exits.* **MAMA** *watches her go and then wheels around and is now* **ETHAN** *chopping wood.*)

AMELIA. Hi.

ETHAN. Hi.

AMELIA. You're going aren't you?

ETHAN. Yes.

AMELIA. I shoulda found myself one of those dandies that dresses up nice and talks about nothing. No fear of one of them up and volunteering.

ETHAN. Amelia.

> (**ETHAN** *tries to take her hand. She pulls away.*)

AMELIA. Or a dull farm boy. Ben Wyatt! Now with Ben I'd be safe. We could just talk about chores and threshing all day long. I'd never have to ask: "Could you leave me something to remember you by?" and "Will we ever see each other again?" and "Oh yeah I sure hope you don't die!"

ETHAN. You know you're kind of spirited when things don't go your way.

> (**AMELIA** *strikes out at* **ETHAN**. *He catches her by the wrist and brings her in close.*)

If it's any consolation Ben Wyatt was right in front of me in line to volunteer. So I don't think you'd have been any better off with him.

AMELIA. I'm sorry I said that about Ben.

> (*Pause.*)

So you're all signed up?

ETHAN. Ben and I are going to serve in the Pennsylvania Volunteers Twentieth Regiment.

AMELIA. Couldn't you ask me first?

ETHAN. I'm sorry.

> (*Pause.*)

What would you have said?

AMELIA. That you should honor your beliefs.

ETHAN. I hope I'm honoring yours as well.

AMELIA. You are.

ETHAN. Well, there you go.

AMELIA. Ethan, thank you.

ETHAN. For what?

AMELIA. For always listening to me.

ETHAN. I try not to miss a word. Mostly 'cause I never know what's coming next.

AMELIA. Will you marry me?

ETHAN. Now see, that right there would be a good example.

>*(Pause.)*

And just so you know that I was listening.

>**(ETHAN** *gets down on one knee.)*

Yes ma'am, I will marry you.

AMELIA. How much time do we have?

ETHAN. Leave tomorrow.

AMELIA. Not much of a honeymoon.

ETHAN. They don't expect it to last more than ninety days. And then we'll be together again.

AMELIA. I'm going to hold you to your word.

ETHAN. You do that. Here I want you to have this. You keep it until I get back.

>**(ETHAN** *takes off a cross from around his neck and puts it on* **AMELIA**.*)*

I love you, Amelia.

>**(AMELIA** *doesn't respond.)*

>*(Covering the silence.)*

It's my mama's silver cross. She gave it to me just before she died.

>*(He begins receding into the dark.)*

It'll keep you safe. We'll see each other soon…

AMELIA. ETHAN!

>**(AMELIA** *is alone.)*

I once told you that nothing scared me. Well I was wrong. You scared me, right to the core. Just before you left you told me you loved me… I didn't say anything.

>*(Pause.)*

I'm thinking on that one long and hard.

I went back to working the dairy tougher than ever. Just trying to stay busy. Always looking for a letter from you.

I know you wrote regular but the letters would come in a clump and then not at all for weeks. I thought I'd go mad waiting.

ETHAN. "My dearest Amelia,

I lay awake in my tent at night and dream of your soft skin and steady heartbeat. You'd think I would sleep soundly with Ben Wyatt right next to me going on about the mill and other stellar subjects but even so most nights I don't sleep for missing you. So far I am in fair condition. I fear disease more than the rebel bullet. We have lost nine men to pneumonia and malaria in the last four months.

I will 'acknowledge the corn' as they say and tell you that I am quickly tiring of hard tack and long for some of your biscuits and gravy. I trust that you are well and not working too hard. That's a joke. I am certain that you are working too hard. The dairy sounds like it is running at the highest efficiency ever. Those poor cows. I hope you will take time to relax on occasion and sit by the brook where we had many happy and unforgettable hours. Yours in abiding love, Ethan."

AMELIA. Started hearing more and more about someone's relative coming back without a leg or worse. The Union defeat at Bull Run left us all dumbstruck. Rebs chased us clean back to D.C.

Had to do something – so I volunteered at the hospital over towards Auburn. You'd been gone almost two years now and just like you I wasn't sleeping much.

There was one fella who came into the hospital without a name. He'd been found at Chancellorsville. Another victory for the South. Stripped by the rebels and left for dead. Far enough from a barrage of canister to survive but close enough to lose his hearing, his sight and part of his jaw. All bandaged up, couldn't even see his face.

> (**AMELIA** *moves to the soldier lying on the ground and holds his hand.*)

AMELIA. Good morning, my friend. It's good to be here with you. I guess you're resting. I'll just set a spell. I wish you could see it outside. It's so crisp and blue out there.

Saw a couple of baby deer cut and run, kicking up their heels.

> *(He moves.)*

Oh, there you are. Good morning!

> *(She gives his hand a squeeze.)*

I hope you had a good rest.

> *(She helps him sit up a bit.)*

There you go, sitting up better. You're getting stronger.

> *(They sit and then the soldier's body starts to shake.)*

Are you alright?

> *(The shaking becomes more violent.)*

Doctor! Are you having a seizure? Doctor!

> *(Finally the soldier is able to grab her wrist.)*

What are you –?

> *(The soldier opens her palm and tries to spell out something in her hand, but it is a huge physical effort.)*

Oh. Oh, my goodness! You're trying to – You're trying to spell!

> *(She grabs his hand and tries to calm him.)*

Why didn't I think of that! Alright, alright we are going to get this. You and me.

> *(She deliberately opens her hand slowly and places his fingers back on her palm.)*

Now let's take this again but nice and slow.

(The soldier's fingers begin to slowly spell across **AMELIA**'s *palm.)*

C – O – L – D! Cold! You're cold! Yes, of course! Here's a blanket. You did it!

(She gets him a blanket. He spells again.)

T – H – A – N – K – Thank you. Oh, you did it!

(She spells back.)

B – L – E – S – S – Y – O – U. Bless you. Oh my goodness. Your name! I need to get your name!

(The soldier grabs her and spells out again, faster and more urgently.)

W – H – E – R – E. Where? You want to know where you are.

(The soldier slumps back.)

Alright, keep it short. P – E – N – N.

(She spells the abbreviation of Pennsylvania for him. His hands move quickly and desperately now.)

W – H – E – R – E. Where. Alright, alright.

(She spells back.)

A – U – B – U – R – N. Auburn.

(He stops her hand and spells.)

I – A – M… I am… B – E – N – W. Ben W.

(The soldier collapses back from the effort.)

Ben Wyatt.

(Pause.)

Ben Wyatt. Ben! Ben!

(She writes in his hand.)

I – A – M…

(He is still.)

AMELIA. No, no, no!

> **(AMELIA** *leans down to check his breath and then, after a long moment, folds his hands on his chest. Pause.)*

My mama and her two sisters could make the most beautiful harmonies together. When my grandma died, they sat with her, held her hand and sang "The Water is Wide" – sang her right into heaven.

I wish I could have sung for Ben. Might have meant something to him. I guess it just wasn't my song to sing.

> *(Pulls blanket over his head and moves away.)*

I hadn't got a letter from you in three months and I was certain this unknown soldier was our own Ben Wyatt. If Ben had been at Chancellorsville then you were there too. The Union lost seventeen thousand in that battle.

You told me this was gonna take ninety days. Two years and three months later and I still got my reply stuck in my throat.

QUARTERMASTER. Yes, ma'am?

AMELIA. I'm trying to find my husband.

QUARTERMASTER. Well he ain't here.

> **(AMELIA** *stares at the clerk.)*

AMELIA. I know that. I am trying to find out where his regiment – the 20th – went after Chancellorsville.

QUARTERMASTER. Ma'am we took a beating in that battle and I spend my whole day trying to get more boots, tents and ammunition to twelve different Pennsylvania regiments. None of which by the way is the 20th. I have no idea. And honestly it's not the kind of information we give out to just anyone. The bestest and onliest way to track your husband's regiment is with the letters you get from him.

AMELIA. I wouldn't be here if I were still getting letters.

QUARTERMASTER. *(Pause.)* Well, ma'am. The best I can do is to tell you to go to the regimental headquarters.

> *(Leans in to her.)*

I might have heard a rumor the 20th is headed toward Gettysburg with General Meade but you didn't hear that from me.

AMELIA. *(Squeezes his hand.)* Thank you.

> **(AMELIA** *exits the scene and starts tiptoeing across the stage.)*

MAMA. Where are you going, Amelia?

AMELIA. Mama, you scared me. What are you doing up in the middle of the night?

MAMA. Worrying about you. You're going after Ethan aren't you?

AMELIA. How'd you know?

MAMA. That's a mother's job. Lay awake at night thinking of the worst things that could happen. Please honey. If you just wait a little longer I'm sure we'll hear from him.

AMELIA. Mama, the clerk said the 20th was headed to *Gettysburg.* That's only a few days' ride. Maggie could do that in her sleep.

MAMA. It's not Maggie I'm worried about. Normally a girl riding by herself across the countryside would give me pause, but during a war I honestly fear for your life. And, well, we don't even know if Ethan… Please don't go Amelia.

AMELIA. I got to Mama. I got to tell him something.

MAMA. And then you'll come right back?

AMELIA. Of course, Mama. Got a dairy to run. You'll see me before the week's out.

MAMA. That would be nice.

> *(Pause.)*

MAMA. And what if he ain't there? You find out they marched off somewhere else? You gonna follow?

> *(Pause.)*

I put a bundle together for you. Biscuits, preserves and some of that boiled ham you like.

AMELIA. You had all that ready?

MAMA. Honey, I been gettin' ready since you faced down that bull. You better go before your daddy wakes up and tries to stop you.

AMELIA. Don't tell him till morning.

MAMA. He knows something's goin' on. Went and got Maggie all shoed up at the blacksmith yesterday.

> *(**MAMA** hugs her and won't let go. **AMELIA** breaks it.)*

You give Ethan a hug from me when you see him.

AMELIA. I promise.

> *(**AMELIA** moves away and into a spotlight.)*

Pure exhilaration – starting an adventure in the middle of the night. Everyone asleep, so quiet, it feels like you're the only one on earth. No more waiting. Maggie and I flew across the countryside and crossed the Susquehanna on the third night.

Gettysburg.

Maggie and I knew we were close. We could hear moans and cries in the night. The musket and artillery smoke now thicker than cotton and stinging my eyes. We came up over a rise. The waxing moon was behind a cloud so you couldn't see anything. And then that cloud moved aside and changed my view of the world forever.

Maggie and I were looking out over a creek. I could see the moonlight bouncing off the water. But as my eyes adapted to the light I realized that this was no creek at all but a field of bodies. And where I had imagined water flowing I could now see that some of the bodies were moving.

They had been passed over for dead and were now becoming conscious again. For the first time I prayed to God that the rebs had captured you back at Chancellorsville.

SAWBONES. *(Flashes an oil lamp.)* Are you the nurse they promised me?

AMELIA. I'm sorry, I'm trying to find the 20th Pennsylvania –

SAWBONES. They're telling me upwards of fifty thousand killed or wounded. In three fucking days. And I get to amputate all of 'em. So you work for me now. Got it?

> *(Pause.)*

Go in that tent and grab my saws and take them down to the creek and clean them. Won't cut anymore they're so filled with bone and gristle. And if you find any whiskey bring it to me.

> *(He hangs the lamp up and freezes.)*

AMELIA. I stumbled in a trance to the creek. Fell to my knees and tried to clean those saws without my stomach turning over. I stayed and helped for three days. I was as likely to come across you here at the field hospital as anywhere else.

It was something terrible. Arms and legs stacked up four foot high like firewood. I kept looking for the right moment to move on and find the 20th but the doc, "Sawbones" they called him, never quit and never gave up on any of those men, so I didn't see how I could.

> *(They are working on a patient.)*

SAWBONES. Looks like a Minié ball in the chest here. Cut away his shirt.

> *(AMELIA cuts away the material. She looks at the patient and stops.)*

AMELIA. Doc.

> *(SAWBONES checks the pulse. AMELIA stares at the patient.)*

SAWBONES. Goddammit. He's gone.

AMELIA. Doc.

SAWBONES. Get him out of here. There's plenty more waiting.

AMELIA. Look again.

SAWBONES. Goddammit, Nurse. Get him out of here.

AMELIA. Don't you mean her?

SAWBONES. *(Takes a good look, pause.)* End of the world has finally come. Fifty thousand and a woman.

AMELIA. How?

SAWBONES. Hell, I don't know. The Army don't make you take your clothes off for the physical so I guess anything is possible.

> *(Pause.)*

Like I said. Get her out of here. If you find any alcohol bring it to me.

> *(**AMELIA** covers the dead woman with a sheet.)*

AMELIA. What were you doing here?

SAWBONES. *(Offstage.)* Nurse!

AMELIA. I finally left the doctor late one night when he collapsed for an hour's drunken rest. One of the wounded said the Pennsylvania 20th had been in the cornfield for part of the battle and that you might still be there. Maggie and I headed off in that direction. Yeah, she was still with me. More than once the doctor had to pull his pistol on someone looking to take off with a beauty like her.

CORP. HAWKINS. *(Very young.)* That's a mighty fine mare you got there, ma'am. If you don't mind, what on earth are you doing riding her through the middle of tarnation?

AMELIA. Trying to find my husband. Looking for the cornfield.

CORP. HAWKINS. You're standing in it. Crossfire so thick, cut it all clean to the ground.

AMELIA. I'm lookin' for the Pennsylvania 20th. A private told me they fought here.

CORP. HAWKINS. They "fought" here? I don't know if I'd call it "fightin'." There was a whole lot of butcherin'. That's what I saw. I never seen so many dead bodies. I didn't know one cannonball could kill four men. That's something new for me. Real interestin'. First man it took his head off his shoulders like it was greased, second man put a hole in his chest you could stick your head through, third man cut him clean in half – that's my friend, Joshua – and the fourth man, more like a boy, tore out his loins. All dead. One cannonball. I ain't never gonna forget that. Hope I do though. You think there's any chance I'll ever get that out of my head?

> *(Pause.* **AMELIA** *sits next to him and takes his hand.)*

They say 200,000 men here. It'll mark every one of us like a cattle brand.

AMELIA. My name is Amelia. Amelia Watson.

CORP. HAWKINS. Corporal Hawkins. Amos Hawkins.

AMELIA. Amos.

CORP. HAWKINS. You say my name so soft – reminds me of my sister. I could imagine her doing something like this.

> *(Pause.)*

She used to do everything I did. Hunting, riding, climbing trees. Oh, God, I wish I could…

> *(Pause.)*

I better get back to it. I'm on burial detail.

AMELIA. I'll keep you in my prayers, Amos.

CORP. HAWKINS. Thank you, ma'am. I'll be needing that.

> *(Pause.)*

Hope you find your husband. Sorry, ma'am, what regiment?

AMELIA. Pennsylvania 20th.

CORP. HAWKINS. 20th. They fought near us on Cemetery Ridge. Brave men. Hit pretty hard. Last I heard they were headed south with Meade towards Virginia.

AMELIA. South?

CORP. HAWKINS. Yes, ma'am.

> *(Pause.)*

Miss Amelia. You should head home and wait for news. Your husband…most of the 20th were killed…he may be –

AMELIA. He's alive. I know it.

CORP. HAWKINS. Yes, ma'am. Any further south… A woman alone on a fresh horse – you can't imagine what –

AMELIA. Amos. Please…just point me down the road they took.

CORP. HAWKINS. I wish you could meet my sister. The road is that direction – you can't miss it. Stay out of sight as much as you can.

AMELIA. Amos was right about not being able to miss the road south. Lined with dead horses and the shoeless bodies of hundreds of rebel soldiers. At one point, the corpses had swamped the road and there was nothing for it but to ride over the top of them, I could feel the bones cracking under Maggie's weight.

These boys, some of 'em just scraps to look at – and they had been holding us to a draw for two years?

Maggie and I are starting to look a little thin. It's been almost ten days since I had a square meal and Maggie can only graze on so much charred grass.

I try to hole up if the moon is out but we also need to make time if we're ever gonna catch up to you. Took us a whole week just to get to the Potomac. Cross the river into Virginia. Smells different here. I stop at a stream to water Maggie.

> *(A rebel stands behind **AMELIA** and points his musket at her.)*

HORSE THIEF. That your horse over there, ma'am? Maggie, I believe?

AMELIA. How do you know her name?

HORSE THIEF. You told me. I been tracking you now for a couple of miles. This full moon is like daylight. Hard to keep up on foot but it was worth it. That's a fine mare. Maggie and I will be leaving together.

(**AMELIA** *moves toward Maggie.*)

You can leave everything in the saddlebags. I'll take care of it for you. If I had more time I'd take care of you as well. Not bad. Sad to say but I got to get back to my company. Wait'll they see my new horse. I'd get moving if I was you. I'll be bringing the company back this way in a few hours I'm sure they'd love to meet you.

AMELIA. Please, sir. I need my horse. Take anything else. Surely horse stealing is still a crime in the Confederate states as well?

HORSE THIEF. Stealing? All of us is way past stealing, ma'am. None of my boys have eaten for weeks 'ceptin' some dog meat and a little rancid corn meal.

(*Grabs her by the throat.*)

Let me tell you a little somethin' about stealin'. Your boys come through my county six months ago and stripped every morsel of food for twenty square mile. Winter comes on quick and babies died. You hear what I'm saying. Babies died from that stealin'. So you got nothing to say to me.

(*Pause.*)

You have a good night, ma'am.

(*He tosses her aside.*)

(*Clucks to Maggie.*) Come on, girl.

(*He exits.* **AMELIA** *is on the ground coughing, trying to breathe again. We hear the loud clap of a hand on a horse's backside.*)

HORSE THIEF. *(Offstage.)* GET UP THERE!

> *(A fast gallop off into the distance.)*

AMELIA. Maggie! My Maggie.

> *(Pause.)*

No horse – I'm a dead woman.

> *(Pause.)*

Come on. Get yourself moving Amelia. Keep to the river and get moving. Reeds cutting at my face. Stumbling in and out of ankle-deep mud, covered in it. Sobbing and making enough noise to bring the whole rebel army.

> *(A man grabs* AMELIA *from behind and covers her mouth. He moves her across the stage and forces her down. He comes face to face with her for the first time. Wipes her face, turns it to the moonlight.)*

SAMUEL. Oh, lord, Samuel. A white woman. What have you done? Now, miss. Ain't no need to be afraid. I'm from over at Master Simmon's plantation just up the road. Heard something and come running – sound like you in trouble. Please, miss. Meant no harm. No harm. Please, miss.

> *(*SAMUEL *slowly removes his hand from her mouth. His hand curls into a fist by his side.)*

AMELIA. Name is Amelia.

> *(She reaches out her hand.* SAMUEL *looks at her hand and then cautiously shakes.)*

SAMUEL. Miss Amelia? Name is Samuel.

> *(Pause.)*

Where you from, miss?

AMELIA. Pennsylvania.

SAMUEL. *(Breathes again.)* Long way from home, miss.

AMELIA. Yes.

SAMUEL. No white woman from around here gonna tell me her first name and try to shake my hand.

AMELIA. No slave from "Master Simmon's plantation" is gonna run around at night trying to rescue strange women on the river bank.

SAMUEL. Yes, miss. Now that we know who we ain't we better get moving before someone figure out who we is.

AMELIA. Samuel ran me through the woods for almost an hour. Finally, we come to a farmhouse. Too dark to see much and it all happened so fast. Down into a root cellar and then a tunnel beneath that. Then, a little room with a mud floor and nothing else.

 (They are both breathing hard.)

SAMUEL. Got one little sweet potato for you.

 *(She snatches it, gulps it down like an animal, licking her fingers. She sees **SAMUEL** watching her and begins to sob.)*

Miss, we can't be having that. Too much noise.

 *(**AMELIA** nods, works to gather herself.)*

AMELIA. I'm sorry. I don't know what's come over me.

SAMUEL. Yes, ma'am.

AMELIA. Where are we? Whose farmhouse?

SAMUEL. Can't really say.

AMELIA. Must be a brave man.

SAMUEL. Or an even braver woman. Said too much.

If I'd seen you was a white woman I'd have left you on that riverbank.

Your face in the shadows – I thought you was runnin' the railway.

 (Pause.)

Why would a white Pennsylvania lady be running along a Virginia river bank in the middle of the night?

AMELIA. Trying to find my husband.

SAMUEL. Yes, ma'am. A soldier?

(*She nods.*)

SAMUEL. I guessed at it. Sometimes, a couple of days after these battles you see some of the most unexpected folks out there trying to find they loved ones. Half these boys can't afford a name pin, army got no way to keep track of the dead, nobody knows for sure who's laying out there. This war – takes they lives and it takes they stories.

AMELIA. He's with the Pennsylvania 20th. Supposed to be on that road next to the river heading south. Woulda caught up to him by now but my horse got stolen. And now…

(**AMELIA** *begins to break down again.*)

SAMUEL. (*Quieting her.*) Yes, ma'am. I understand.

AMELIA. No you don't. I'm…fearless.

SAMUEL. Yes, ma'am…I hear the word "fearless" and sometimes I think "stupid." Maybe "scared" is the smart thing now you got something to lose…

AMELIA. I don't know how I'm gonna find him.

SAMUEL. One thing I can say about this war is that it is extraordinary. I seen all manner of extraordinary good and tenfold bad. Seems to bring out the extraordinary in everyone. You'll find him, ma'am, I know you will.

AMELIA. How?

SAMUEL. You make a way. You might not be fearless anymore, but I bet you find some courage.
That's when you go ahead even if you scared out yo' mind.
I know it's hard. All alone. My whole family. Taken, sold. But I know if they out there I'm gonna find 'em.

AMELIA. You out there by the river, every night?

(**SAMUEL** *nods.*)

Looking for them?

SAMUEL. Yes, ma'am. Them and anyone else come along the route.

AMELIA. Are you scared?

SAMUEL. Every damn time.

AMELIA. You should head north. This is not safe for you.

SAMUEL. *(Amused.)* Yes, ma'am, I'm sure you right.

AMELIA. You know, my husband, Ethan. He's fighting for you.

SAMUEL. Ma'am?

AMELIA. Ethan volunteered. First day. He's fighting to end slavery.

SAMUEL. Ethan must be an extraordinary man.

(*Pause.*)

All due respect, ma'am, but from what I see that ain't what this war is about. I'm pretty sure all them big men up in Washington don't want to lose half of they land and all the cotton that comes with it. All this blood being spilt by white men? Ain't for no black man, but for that "white gold."

AMELIA. Yes. I'm sorry.

You just want your family and I just want Ethan.

SAMUEL. That's the truth, ma'am.

AMELIA. Amelia, Samuel.

SAMUEL. Miss Amelia. You better sleep while you can. So we can find Mr. Ethan.

AMELIA. We?

SAMUEL. I'll get you as far south as I can tomorrow night and then hole up at the next hideaway. That is, if you still plan on going south?

AMELIA. *(Pause.)* I...I don't know...my mama and daddy...

SAMUEL. Yes, ma'am...and no horse.

(*Pause.*)

What you think Ethan would say?

AMELIA. "Go home. It's too dangerous."

SAMUEL. Yes, ma'am.

*(They share a long look. **AMELIA** finally cannot meet his gaze.)*

SAMUEL. Yes, ma'am.

*(Lights slowly fade as **AMELIA** buries her face in her arms. **SAMUEL** stays upright, still on watch. There is a long pause and then **AMELIA** finally speaks in the dark.)*

AMELIA. Samuel?

SAMUEL. Yes, ma'am?

AMELIA. I usually do the opposite of what Ethan says.

SAMUEL. Yes, ma'am. I'll take you south after dark.

AMELIA. Thank you. Thank you.

SAMUEL. Miss Amelia.

AMELIA. Yes, Samuel.

SAMUEL. Go to sleep.

*(**SAMUEL** clambers back up into the tunnel above.)*

AMELIA. Good to his word Samuel ran me all the next night heading south. On at least five occasions I thought my heart would burst we ran so hard.

*(**SAMUEL** is lying downstage right staring out into the audience. Faint sound of an army marching, approaching.)*

SAMUEL. Miss Amelia. Down here.

*(**AMELIA** lies down next to him.)*

I believe that right there is the Army of the Potomac moving fast. I best go before the sun get any higher. Maybe Mr. Ethan come along any minute. Here this is for you.

*(**AMELIA** unfolds a piece of paper. **SAMUEL** takes off down the center aisle and into the darkness.)*

AMELIA. Money! Samuel I can't take –

*(**AMELIA** looks around. The marching sound grows.)*

I look out at that endless line of soldiers. All those stone-cut faces.

Excuse me, sir? Have you seen the Pennsylvania 20th Volunteers? Sir?

(Runs down the line trying again.)

Sir, have you seen the Pennsylvania 20th Volunteers? HAS ANYONE SEEN THE PENNSYLVANIA 20TH?! Please someone help me.

(A voice rings out from the dark of the audience.)

DEAD EYES. Hey, gal.

(AMELIA stops, strains to see out into the audience.)

AMELIA. Hello? Who's there?

DEAD EYES. Down here in the railroad cut.

AMELIA. I can't see you. I'm looking for the Pennyslvania 20th.

DEAD EYES. Yeah, gal. I seen 'em. Fought alongside the 20th.

AMELIA. What? Oh my lord, you have to help me. Where did you see them? When?

DEAD EYES. PENN – SLY – VAY – NEE – UH.

(He laughs to himself.)

AMELIA. Sir, please. Can you come out where I can see you?

DEAD EYES. No, gal. Can't come out in that sunlight, you got to come down here, you wants the 20th.

AMELIA. Uh, well, I don't see a path, how do I…

DEAD EYES. Just a few feet in front of you. Come on down. I ain't gonna bite. Come on down, gal. Step careful, some of them stones is loose. That's it. Come on down. That's it.

> *(She still can't see him and neither can most of the audience, they just hear his voice. He's out there somewhere, hunkered down in the dark. She carefully climbs off the stage and out into the*

unknown. She's halfway down the aisle when he rises up.)

DEAD EYES. Hey gal.

AMELIA. Oh god!

(They come face to face. She turns away immediately.)

DEAD EYES. What's wrong? You looking at my burns?

AMELIA. *(Still averting her face.)* No sir.

(He reaches out, puts his hands on her, pulls her in.)

DEAD EYES. Yeah, you is. Now you's close enough I reckon you can smell it too.

AMELIA. I'm sorry it must hurt something terrible.

DEAD EYES. Oh yeah they's burnin', they's burnin' like a flame is on it right now.

AMELIA. My arm, you're hurting me.

(He is all over her now, holding her.)

DEAD EYES. Johnny reb come at me, flames coming off his head like a torch, licking at my face.

(A bugle call interrupts. He stiffens and listens.)

That's my call. Got to report.

(He is backing away from her, heading down the aisle. She staggers up and lunges at him. Now she is clutching him.)

AMELIA. Wait. You said you knew something about the 20th.

DEAD EYES. Gal, you best get off me!

(He shrugs her off.)

AMELIA. No, no. You said you seen 'em. You tell me.

(They are face to face again.)

DEAD EYES. Can't be out in this sunlight. Got to report.

AMELIA. You promised me. I come down here in the dark... you damn well better tell me something.

DEAD EYES. I don't got to tell you nothing.

> *(Bugle sounds again. He tries to shake her off, she is all over him.)*

AMELIA. I know what they do. I know what they do – you desert, they even think you deserted. You'll be sittin' on the edge of your own casket.

DEAD EYES. Let me go – can't be late!

AMELIA. You ain't goin' nowhere until you tell me. The 20th?! Pennsylvania?

DEAD EYES. At Gettysburg, fought alongside us. Most are dead, the rest captured.

AMELIA. What? Boy at Gettysburg didn't say anything about "captured"!

DEAD EYES. Killed or captured. They's overrun by the rebs. If they ain't dead they's prisoners.

> *(She slackens her grip. He starts to scramble away, she grabs him again.)*

AMELIA. Where?

DEAD EYES. What?

AMELIA. Where did they go? Where did they take the prisoners?

> *(Bugle sounds again.)*

DEAD EYES. I don't know, I don't know! Most go to Danville, but I hear that's full up. Building a big new prison in Georgia. Andersonville.

AMELIA. How do I get there?

DEAD EYES. Where?

AMELIA. Andersonville.

DEAD EYES. You don't. Only ones going to Andersonville is Union soldiers, prisoners of war.

> *(He breaks **AMELIA**'s grip and turns to run – a loud cannon boom…and then – a smiling **ETHAN** lying on the ground. They are at a picnic, the sound of a brook slowly rises.)*

ETHAN. I got you figured, you know.

AMELIA. Ethan?

> (**AMELIA**, *dazed, stares out front.*)

ETHAN. Oh, I love it when you say my name.

> (**AMELIA** *slowly recognizes her place in this flashback.*)

AMELIA. I remember this… I don't think I can… I have to go…

ETHAN. You don't have to go yet, the dairy will wait. Like I was saying – I got you figured.

AMELIA. What do you mean?

ETHAN. You want everyone to think you're so tough.

> (*That stops her.*)

AMELIA. That's 'cause I am.

ETHAN. Oh yeah, you're a pretty hard case, I guess, when you want to be. But why are you always trying to prove it?

AMELIA. 'Cause no man, especially the boys at the dairy, will ever take you serious if you don't show a little grit.

ETHAN. I do.

AMELIA. Well, Ethan… That's probably why I'm here with you – when I should be back at the dairy.

> (*He thinks for a moment and then begins piecing together an improvised song for her.*)

ETHAN.

AMELIA… AMELIA, SHE'LL STEAL YOUR HEART AWAY,
AMELIA, AMELIA, AS FRESH AS A BRAND NEW DAY,
SHE'S CUTE, PETITE,
AND OH SO SWEET, TO HOLD HER IS BEYOND COMPARE,
BUT DON'T CONFUSE HER WITH A DAINTY GIRL – YOU'RE
HOLDING A GRIZZLY BEAR!

> (*She laughs, in spite of herself, and then tries to hit him. He grabs her arms. She pins him to the ground.*)

AMELIA. Ethan! You take that back!

ETHAN. What? The part about your being cute?

AMELIA. *(Laughing.)* Take it back!

ETHAN. Okay! So, you're not petite!

AMELIA. You know what I mean!

(She moves away, genuinely hurt.)

ETHAN. Awwww. The grizzly bear? That part?

(She gives a little nod.)

Aw, honey. I'm sorry. Just trying to make you laugh.

(Pause.)

Amelia?

(She ignores him.)

(Softly.)

AMELIA, AMELIA, A GRIZZLY BEAR – SHE'S NOT…
AMELIA, AMELIA, MY BEATING HEART SHE'S GOT…
SHE'S THE ONLY ONE I EVER MET THAT COULD REACH
   RIGHT TO MY SOUL,
AMELIA, AMELIA, MY DARLING YOU'VE MADE ME WHOLE…

(She smiles to herself and then slowly turns… They come together.)

Amelia, I love you.

(Pause.)

AMELIA. I…

(Pause.)

(Another cannon boom, similar to the beginning of the scene but now much louder. She pulls away scared and jumps up.)

That was close!

(ETHAN *is frozen in place. She looks at him and slowly, lovingly reaches out and touches his face.)*

Ethan? Ethan?

(Lights slowly fade on ETHAN. AMELIA *stumbles downstage.)*

*(We hear a distant bugle playing "Taps." * AMELIA *slowly recovers, coming back into the present.)*

AMELIA. That's the signal – end of day, no more fighting. I head onto that moonlit battlefield, keeping one eye peeled for hogs that come after the dead bodies – hell, live bodies if you're in their way. All the time stepping over corpses and praying not to see your lifeless face staring up.

I was now truly starving. Samuel's sweet potato had only served to torture. I was in a hateful cycle of short bouts of sleep and hallucinations.

VERMONT. I'm here.

AMELIA. *(Frightened.)* Who are you?

VERMONT. Don't you know? You've been avoiding me – but I'm the perfect choice. Just about your size. Recently dispatched so I'm not so bloated you can't get the uniform off. Way out here in the woods where no one'll see you.

AMELIA. No.

VERMONT. There's no other way.

AMELIA. But how can I?

VERMONT. Ethan.

AMELIA. I can't do that to you.

VERMONT. It's all yours. Musket, money, ammunition box. I won't need any of it. The regiment, my family – they'll never find me here – hidden away in this oak scrub. How about that? I even managed to die in an unassuming manner.

AMELIA. I'm not a grave robber.

VERMONT. You know it's not grave robbing. What's stopping you?

AMELIA. After all this time, if I ever find him… I don't want to become a man. How will Ethan know me?

VERMONT. Ethan has always known you. That's what brought you this far.

(**AMELIA** *picks up* **VERMONT***'s musket.*)

I know your daddy taught you how to use that musket. But that bayonet? Well – that's one for you to figure.

(**VERMONT** *disappears as* **AMELIA** *stares at the bayonet. After a moment of thought, she starts to cut off her hair with it as the lights fade. Lights up elsewhere on a severely wounded* **COLONEL**.*)

COLONEL. *(On his last legs.)* Listen up, boys. Got some news. I've received notice that they're gonna break up our regiment make it part of an outpost in South Carolina. According to this order, this piece of paper…we've "lost too many to function." They do not understand the exceptional bravery of you men to fight on for the last few months…an act of greatness…
I told myself at the beginning of all this to think of each of you as a son, so that I would always remember the precious lives I was responsible for. To lose so many of my children is…
Report to Sergeant Davis for your orders.

(**AMELIA** *slowly approaches the* **COLONEL** *in her Union blue uniform.*)

AMELIA. Captain?

(He grabs his shoulder patch.)

COLONEL. Colonel!

AMELIA. *(Keeping her head down.)* Colonel. Yes, sir. I got separated from my regiment and they're long gone. Could I volunteer myself for this march south, sir?

COLONEL. Do whatever you like.

AMELIA. I'm sure those boys know you tried to keep them safe.

COLONEL. We'll never know.

AMELIA. Yes, sir.

(Salutes him.)

AMELIA. Thank you, sir.

(**AMELIA** *moves off.*)

A long, hard march. Two weeks and we cross into South Carolina. When I'm not thinking about you I'm thinking about food. Seen a farmhouse in the distance about a half mile back and as we set camp I strike out towards it before dark.

(Knocking.) Hello, anybody home?

(No answer, walks in.)

Hello?

This was a nice farmhouse once. It could have been ours back home. But then you could see a couple of the windows were shot out, half-covered with oilcloth pieces too small to do the job and the tell-tale signs that critters were coming and going as they pleased.

MRS. SULLIVAN. *(Pokes her head out, carrying a shotgun.)* We ain't got nothing. Go away.

AMELIA. I mean you no harm. Just hoping to buy some food.

MRS. SULLIVAN. That's one I ain't heard before.

AMELIA. Ma'am?

MRS. SULLIVAN. Offering to buy food. If I had any food don't you think I'd give it to my boy before I'd sell it to you?

AMELIA. A boy pokes his head out from the kitchen. All eyes and bones.

(Pause.)

Yes, ma'am. Sorry to disturb you, ma'am.

MRS. SULLIVAN. What kind of yank offers to pay for his food? Awful polite for a yank. Where you from?

AMELIA. Pennsylvania, ma'am.

MRS. SULLIVAN. Uh.

AMELIA. Sorry to bother you, ma'am.

(AMELIA starts to go.)

MRS. SULLIVAN. Got a good well, though.

AMELIA. Ma'am?

MRS. SULLIVAN. If you wanted to buy some fresh water.

AMELIA. Yes please, ma'am. Thank you, ma'am. How much for a glass?

MRS. SULLIVAN. Oh, I'll just get it for you. Felt like a fool even saying it. Thomas, go and get this boy a glass of water.

AMELIA. I seen a cow. Could you sell me some milk?

MRS. SULLIVAN. That cow is worse starving than us. She dried up long time ago. Me and the boy just wait on the two chickens to give us an egg every few days. That's all we got. First our boys in gray took all the corn and then you yanks took all the cattle 'ceptin' that milk cow. Hid her in my bedroom when I seen 'em coming.

AMELIA. Your husband?

MRS. SULLIVAN. Fighting. Been gone for three years. Begged him not to go. If your boys don't get him – I probably will.
(Pause.) Let me ask you something. Who is this war helping?

AMELIA. Yes, ma'am.

MRS. SULLIVAN. We're both starving. It ain't doing you or me no good. You seen our boys? No shoes or hats, barely a shirt on their back. My husband has been paid exactly twice for his three years of service in the Confederate Army. They's burnin' acorns for coffee. Where's this all gonna end up?

AMELIA. I don't know.

MRS. SULLIVAN. Well I don't either. What's it going to prove? How insane we all are?
(Pause.)
You're about the prettiest, most delicate-featured boy I've ever seen. Can't believe you made for fighting.

(Pause.)

MRS. SULLIVAN. Where is that boy? THOMAS!

*(**MRS. SULLIVAN** exits.)*

AMELIA. I didn't see much point in staying. Seemed like she was on to me. I left a little money for them.
Toilsome marching for four more days and into the fort.

COL. BINDER. Gentlemen, my name is Colonel Binder. Welcome to Fort Wagner. Sergeant Davis will give you your orders and get you familiar with our routines. I am also soliciting volunteers from our already stationed men for a special mission south of here.

AMELIA. *(Salutes.)* Yes, sir. I volunteer sir.

COL. BINDER. Admirable soldier, admirable. But you've just come off a forced march with no food. Won't allow it.

AMELIA. Sir. I am ready and a sure shot!

COL. BINDER. Did I ask you to speak, soldier?

(Stares at her.)

You Fort Wagner "boys" might want to take a look right now.

Right over here. This is what a "man" looks like. Weeks of forced march on two bites of hard tack and he's got the best of you in his first day here. What's your name soldier?

AMELIA. Private Miller, sir.

COL. BINDER. Miller. Honor to meet you sir. Sergeant Davis, see that Private Miller here gets double rations before heading south. DISMISSED!

*(**COL. BINDER** exits.)*

AMELIA. Quite pleased with myself! Heading further south *and* getting some quality food in my belly! A whole mess of drumfish, whatever that is, soaked in buttermilk and goldenfried in cornmeal. Mmmm-hmmm, all to myself. Army life ain't all bad.

(Laughs at herself.)

Must be crazy. Heading south for worse and worse. I just got to tell you something.

*(**BALTIMORE** interrupts her reverie.)*

BALTIMORE. Hey, Fresh Fish!

*(**AMELIA** slowly takes **BALTIMORE** in.)*

AMELIA. What?

BALTIMORE. You ready?

AMELIA. *(Salutes.)* Yes, sir.

BALTIMORE. No need to call me sir. Just a private like you. Well not exactly like you. As Colonel Binder explains it I guess I'm half the man you are.

(Sound of detail marching.)

Come on!

(They march out and around the audience during this conversation.)

The sergeant asked me to partner up with you on the march to our "special" mission. Baltimore's the name.

AMELIA. Miller.

BALTIMORE. Oh, I know your name. You're already famous at the fort for volunteering for one of Colonel Binder's "special" missions.

AMELIA. Didn't you volunteer?

BALTIMORE. Are you kidding me? No one's ever volunteered.

AMELIA. Why not.

BALTIMORE. 'Cause it's the same damn mission every time. A pissant little bridge we've been trading hands with the graybacks over. One side takes it, a bunch of us die, few months later, same thing all over again.

AMELIA. Why does he keep sending you out?

BALTIMORE. Wants to make a name for himself. Wants everyone to know that he's the big toad in the puddle.

    (Pause.)

BALTIMORE. You know you look pretty soft for someone who volunteered for this kind of duty. You sure you ain't going to see the elephant in this little brawl?

AMELIA. What do you mean?

BALTIMORE. Shit. I guess you answered my question.

    *(**BALTIMORE** grabs **AMELIA** and shoves her against a wall, gesturing for the others to march on.)*

"Seeing the elephant" means going into battle for the first time! You telling me you never heard that before?

AMELIA. Guess I didn't hear you right.

BALTIMORE. Uh-huh. Can you shoot that musket? 'Cause if not we can part ways right now.

AMELIA. How many cartridges in my ammunition box?

BALTIMORE. Forty. Same for everyone.

AMELIA. *(Stares him down.)* Then, that's forty dead rebs by my count.

BALTIMORE. *(Laughs.)* I hope you shoot as good as you talk.

    (Deadly serious.)

You keep your head down, do what I tell you, got it?

    *(**AMELIA** nods. **BALTIMORE** laughs.)*

Forty dead rebs!

    (Shouts.)

Hey, sarge! You gotta hear this one.

    (Runs ahead.)

AMELIA. Ridiculous thing to say, of course. I didn't plan on shooting anyone. But if I was going to survive the battle I knew I needed someone like Baltimore by my side.

BALTIMORE. Fresh Fish, stay down and get over here!

    *(**BALTIMORE** is hunkered down behind the stone wall of the bridge.)*

(Peeks over the wall.) You see that line of oak trees? They'll more than likely be coming through there.

(Starts loading his musket.)

You ever hear a chargin' line of graybacks do that holler?

AMELIA. Don't know what you mean.

BALTIMORE. They don't call it seeing the elephant for nothing.

(For everyone's benefit.) You better suck up your balls nice and tight and get ready for the most exciting turkey shoot you ever been on.

>*(**BALTIMORE** watches for the rebs. **AMELIA** stays down, hiding behind the wall, listening. **BALTIMORE** wheels and drops below the wall.)*

Shit! I seen something! They're out there.

>*(Musket fire explodes around them. **BALTIMORE** is up and firing. The action goes slomo – He drops down to re-load, bellowing at **AMELIA**, who is not moving. We cannot hear **BALTIMORE**'s shouts, and then finally back to normal speed and sound.)*

Get up. Fire your goddamn musket. Get up and fire.

>*(**AMELIA** fires wildly.)*

Not at the goddamn trees!

>*(**AMELIA** drops and re-loads.)*

Take a breath you stupid sonofabitch!

>*(**AMELIA** breathes, takes good aim, and fires. They both watch for a long moment in silence and then…)*

AMELIA. I hit him.

BALTIMORE. He ain't getting up! You done him.

AMELIA. He looked like Ethan.

>*(Battle sounds come back up and **BALTIMORE** slaps a dazed **AMELIA** on the shoulder.)*

BALTIMORE. Hey! Fresh Fish you weren't kidding about that ammunition box was you! That was one heck of a shot!

> *(Checks over the wall.)*

Whoooaaa. Look at that shit! A fucking wall of fog. All them muskets firing at the same time'll do that. Goddamn.

I can't see two feet. Okay, so next charge we got a whole new set of problems. All this smoke we're gonna be firing blind. If you can see a leg below the smoke line shoot at that. If you see a musket flare fire at that. You'd be surprised how many you can hit. Just don't get turned around in the fog or you'll be shooting at me. Got it?

> *(Pause.)*

It's better this way. You won't see who you hit. You alright?

> *(Pause.)*

Yeah, it'll get you that way for a while. It's something to think on, ain't it?

> *(Pause.)*

Well, you done good. Your daddy'll be real proud. I don't think I could've hit the side of a barn my first time I had the shakes so bad.

> *(Pause.)*

This is some shit ain't it?

> *(Quiet and then much louder sounds of musket fire.)*

Stay down. They got close! Bastards snuck up in the smoke.

> *(A bugle sounds in the distance.)*

Shit. That's the retreat signal. Well, you made it. Seen your elephant. Let's go! Stay low and head straight back.

(**AMELIA** *does not move.* **BALTIMORE** *gets moving, looks back.*)

Goddammit! Didn't you hear me?

(**BALTIMORE** *looks over the wall, ducks a bullet.*)

What's wrong? Are you hit?

AMELIA. *(Calm.)* I'm alright.

BALTIMORE. *(Abandoning her.)* Shit! You're crazy.

(**AMELIA** *watches* **BALTIMORE** *go and then tosses her musket aside and waits. A rebel comes over the wall in silhouette.*)

(*He rears back his musket and hits her in the mouth with the butt of the gun. Blackout.*)

(*Sound of wagon wheels and horses comes up. There is a* **DRIVER** *sitting above* **AMELIA.** *She is out cold.*)

DRIVER. Hey, little yank. You coming around? Welcome to the confederacy!

(*The light on the* **DRIVER** *fades out and comes back up.*)

That jaw don't look too good, lil' yank. One of our boys whomped you a piece.

(*Lights fade and come up again.*)

Hey! Got twenty thousand of you in the battle of the Wilderness! Roll, Alabama, roll! You don't look so good! They're sending boys to do a man's job. Boys!

(*Lights fade and come up again as the wagon lurches to a halt.*)

Whooaa!

AMELIA. How long have I been out?

DRIVER. Long enough you need to ask. Stopping here for a moment, lil' yank. There's some good blackberries just off the road here. Gonna keep your chains on but I'll let you go pick some. If you try anything I'll shoot you dead. Alright? We got a deal? Don't make me shoot you!

AMELIA. Where we headed?

DRIVER. Camp Sumter.

AMELIA. No! I need to get to Andersonville, Georgia.

DRIVER. You hear this one? You need to get to –! Ha, ha! Case you haven't noticed you're a prisoner of the Confederacy. You don't got shit to say! "I need to get to Georgia"!

AMELIA. You have to listen to me. I have some money. Please I have to get to Andersonville.

DRIVER. Huh.

> *(Pause.)*

How much you got?

> (**AMELIA** *reaches into one of her boots and pulls out a small wad of money.*)

Pretty good, pretty good.

AMELIA. You'll take me then?

DRIVER. Yeah…alright.

AMELIA. Thank you for your kindness.

DRIVER. Still got to go to Camp Sumter first.

AMELIA. How far from there to Andersonville?

DRIVER. Just a few feet.

AMELIA. What?

DRIVER. Camp Sumter is about all there is to Andersonville, Georgia!

> *(The* **DRIVER** *bursts out into a huge laugh.)*

You better get moving if you want some of them berries. Probably the last decent food you'll ever see. I'd savor it if I was you. Thanks for the greenbacks! "I gotta get to Andersonville"! Oh yeah. You going to Andersonville. Hey! I bet you is the first yank that paid to get in there! Ha, ha, ha!

(Angry.) Ya other pieces of shit get back on the wagons.

AMELIA. Thank goodness I held back on giving him all my money.

DRIVER. All right, all you bluebellies out! Welcome to Camp Sumter. I hope you enjoy your stay! These fine sons of the Confederacy will escort you the rest of the way!

> (**AMELIA** *moves in direction that the* **DRIVER** *points. The* **DRIVER** *grabs her by the shoulder and pulls her next to him.*)

Hold up there, lil' yank. I'll do all the talkin'.

> (*Shouts.*)

This one's on my work detail. Colonel back in the Carolinas said I could have him. Ain't much to look at, but he'll do for my needs.

AMELIA. What are you doing?

DRIVER. Ain't the time to argue, lil' yank. Just get in the wagon!

AMELIA. I'm not going anywhere. You don't understand.

DRIVER. No, you don't understand. You cannot go in there. Unspeakable. You won't survive. You come with me.

> (*Shouts off.*)

No, he's coming with me. Yes, sir!

> (*Hissing.*)

Goddammit! I'm trying to help you. I'll let you off a few miles from here in the woods, take off your chains. Get it? So shut the fuck up and get in the wagon.

AMELIA. I'm not getting in the wagon.

DRIVER. You do not know what you're doing. There's already thirty thousand men in that outhouse and more coming. It's only built to hold ten. It's the most godforsaken thing I've ever seen.

> (*Pause.*)

If you walk through those gates there'll be cutthroats waiting to take apart a little sawed-off thing like you.

They'll strip you, leave you naked and half dead. Raiders
is what they call 'em – savage as a meat-axe.

Worst place I ever seen and I fought at Cold Harbor –
saw seven thousand men go down in half an hour. This
is worse. You understand? Worse.

AMELIA. *(Shaking.)* I understand…but I'm going anyway.

DRIVER. You can't imagine what you are doing.

> *(Pause.)*

Alright that's it.

> *(Shakes his head in disbelief.)*

You will never forget this moment I promise you.

> *(Shouts off.)*

Aw, hell, take him. Tried to steal my money!

> *(He gives **AMELIA** a shove with his boot. He moves
> away.)*

Watch out for yourself, lil' yank.

> *(Pause, puts his head down.)*

Goddammit.

AMELIA. I'm last to get in line. They take off our chains
and push us in as a group. I can barely feel my legs I'm
shaking so hard.

> *(The massive gate THUDS closed.)*

Walking in here – it's like descending into your own
muddy grave. It's an enclosure in the same way a pig-
sty is. No roof, no shelter. Just a fifteen foot high pine
fence to surround the misery.

There are bodies lying face down in the mud. No one
seems to notice. All those slumped men staring at me.
They're waiting for something.

A terrifying scream and then from all sides they come
charging at a full sprint. They're big and carry crude
wooden clubs. If they strip me, it'll be so much worse
than I can even imagine. Most of the men in front of

me just drop to the ground, bawling for mercy. The brutes fall on them like wolves ripping open a fresh kill.

It's now or never. I take off at a dead run. The biggest raider notices my mad dash and catches me face to face and raises me up. At the full height of his lift I grab his head and drive my forehead into his. Blinding pain. A shout goes up from the men – the crack of our two heads has been so loud. My man falls to his knees.

I stagger off towards that gray mass of men. I disappear into the crowd and collapse into the waste-filled mud of Andersonville.

(Blackout.)

*(***KETCHAM*** *kneels next to* **AMELIA**, *who is just coming to. His one arm is withered.)*

KETCHAM. *(Smiles.)* You're a tiny mule but you got a big kick.

(Pause.)

What you done to that big raider, Morton…

(Clicks his tongue.)

That's the one thing I didn't know.

(He offers her water. **AMELIA** *turns her head away.)*

It's okay to drink – we got a well. No, really! You wouldn't believe what we prisoners get up to. We just dug straight down with sticks and whatnot and well eventually you hit the water line. It's a sight better than that stream runnin' through the middle of the stockade that every man, animal and reb has pissed into.

AMELIA. How long have I been…

KETCHAM. Lying here? Three days. You put a powerful hurt on Morton but on yourself too. That jaw of yours don't look so good neither.

(Pause.)

Name's Ketcham.

AMELIA. Amel…

(Stops herself, pause.)

AMELIA. Miller. Private Miller.

KETCHAM. Take it slow there Miller. You got a nice bump on your head so you just take it easy.

*(**AMELIA** stares up at the tent roof.)*

Ohh, ya lookin' at my roof? Sewed them shirts together myself. This here's a genuine Andersonville Shebang. *(Pause.)* Where you from?

AMELIA. Pennsylvania.

KETCHAM. *(Laughs.)* Not the state, your regiment.

AMELIA. Pennsylvania 20th Volunteers.

KETCHAM. We got some "20" boys around here and some "Bucktails," too. So crowded now. Lord knows where they got to.

AMELIA. *(Sits up.)* I'm looking for one in particular. Ethan Johnson.

KETCHAM. Don't recall an Ethan. Definitely met some boys from the "20" though. This Ethan your friend or someone you tracking down for other reasons?

AMELIA. My best friend.

KETCHAM. Place like this you never know. They's doing evil as much as they's doing good. Half of 'em lost they minds. Hell, I coulda met Ethan but he don't even know his own name anymore. I seen that more than once. Leaders of men stumbling around naked as Eden.

*(**KETCHAM** sees the look of horror on **AMELIA**'s face.)*

Of course, I probably just ain't met this Ethan.

(Pause.)

You don't have any money do yeh?

*(**AMELIA** tries to back away from **KETCHAM** with some effort.)*

Don't worry. I ain't trying to take it.

(Pause.)

Look, you're in real bad shape and the rations here well…you can't last more than a couple of weeks on what they give you. And you gotta be able to walk to get that pitiful ration anyhow.

But if you got money – you can get some real food that'll give you a chance.

(Pause.)

If you want I'll try to get you something with your money. I know it's hard to believe but you can trust me.

*(**AMELIA** takes a long, hard look and then slowly reaches into her left boot.)*

AMELIA. Three dollars.

KETCHAM. No, no. Just one dollar. You're gonna have to make that last. It ain't much but it's a sight better than starving to death. I'll see what I can do.

*(**KETCHAM** exits the tent.)*

MORTON. Ketcham! Get over here you one-armed piece of shit!

What you got there? How did a little shit-eater like you get the wampum to pay for a feast like this?

*(Grabs something out of **KETCHAM**'s bag.)*

Nice. I'll take that. Well, if you insist, I'll take the whole thing. Thanks, old man! So I'll ask again – how'd you pay for all this? What's that? You won it over at the gambling tent?

(Laughs.)

Ketcham I know you to pieces. You forget ol' Morton here served with you in the New York 22nd? I remember you used to carry a bible around with you like it was your baby. I find it hard to believe you were gambling. Where'd you get that kind of cash? Lay down. You heard me, get on the ground. Lay your head on that plank. Now I'm just gonna put my boot on your head and you let me know when you feel like talking. Don't you move! It's funny. You being such a good Christian and all but where is your god now? It turns out I'm the closest thing to God you got here in Andersonville.

(Speaks to the gathering crowd.)

Listen up everyone! You see this shiny lump on my head? Well this fresh meat no bigger than a drummer boy give that to me in front of everyone and I aims to return the favor with a proper Andersonville welcome. Whoever's giving shelter to that little fucker can count on being dead by sundown if they don't give him up. That wouldn't be you would it? A good Christian like you?

*(**MORTON** leans hard on **KETCHAM**'s head with his boot.)*

What's that sound? Is that your skull cracking? I'd talk if I was you. Something's definitely cracking. OH, YOUR shebang? Now that wasn't so hard was it? Awww, bawlin' like a little baby.

(Pause.)

Ketcham if there's one thing I've learned to count on here at Camp Sumter it's that a man will pretty much do anything to save his own skin. Thanks, old man.

*(**MORTON** gets in a good kick and then drops on all fours and starts crawling into **KETCHAM**'s tent as the lights change.)*

AMELIA. I'm lying in my favorite field of wildflowers back home, the smell of sweet pea everywhere and here you come bringing a picnic basket.

*(Suddenly **MORTON**'s hands are choking **AMELIA**. He strains and lifts her off the ground while choking her – and they freeze.)*

Can't believe it ends like this. I'm going fast and all I can do is stare at this roof made of shirts. There's that collar label with something handwritten on it I can never read. That big raider knows I'm close to death and shifts his weight to finish the job. Bumps the tentpole. Moves that collar label a little closer. I can read it now. E…Johnson. Want to shout, tell someone. Think I see Ketcham.

> (**MORTON** *tries to look behind him, then his head jerks forward from a blow accompanied by a sound. He releases his grip on* **AMELIA**. *They both go down in slow motion. Blackout.*)

> (*Lights come up on* **KETCHAM** *holding a prone* **AMELIA**. *He is rocking and whispering over her. After a moment,* **AMELIA** *slowly comes to. She holds her throat and coughs.*)

KETCHAM. Forgive me. Forgive me, Miller. I betrayed you.

AMELIA. *(Barely able to make a sound.)* What?

> (*Pause, looks around.*)

Is Morton dead?

> (**KETCHAM** *nods silently.*)

Where?

KETCHAM. Down the well and all covered up.

> (**AMELIA** *nods.*)

Don't know why I did that. It won't do us any good. They'll figure out soon enough what happened even without his body and now we got no well to boot. We're dead men.

> (*Pause.*)

I'm so sorry for it to end like this, Miller. I made it worse by coming after Morton but I just couldn't –

> (**AMELIA** *suddenly grabs him.*)

AMELIA. The shirt!

KETCHAM. What?

AMELIA. There! The shirt!

> (**AMELIA** *points up to the shirt label.*)

Ethan Johnson. You must have known him!

KETCHAM. *(Looks, pause.)* E. Johnson. No, I'm sure… No Ethan Johnson.

AMELIA. He must have been here at some time!

KETCHAM. *(Desperate.)* I don't know.

AMELIA. *(Calm.)* Ketcham. I don't have much time…

> *(Pause.)*

I didn't come all this way to…

> **(AMELIA** *starts to sob.)*

KETCHAM. I'm sorry, I'm sorry, I betrayed you.

AMELIA. *(Holds his face.)* Listen to me, Ketcham!

> *(Pause.)*

Ethan Johnson is my husband. I have given up everything, including my womanhood, to walk into this prison and find Ethan.

> *(Pause.)*

You have to remember how you got that shirt.

> **(KETCHAM** *stares at her, thinks, finally shakes his head.)*

Maybe he helped you build this tent?

KETCHAM. What's your name? Your real name.

AMELIA. Amelia.

KETCHAM. Oh my lord in heaven. It's that singing boy. Never knew his name. It must have been him. Lived somewhere over that way. He'd always be singing your name.

> *(Pause.)*

One day he come by and seen my shebang I was building. I just got here, scared out of my mind and he says, "You ain't gonna get much cover with only two shirts." Right then and there he takes his shirt off and give it to me. I says, "I can't take that!" He rolls up his pant leg – whole leg turned black. Says, "I won't need it much longer anyway."

(Pause, to himself.)

Singing boy. If he's anywhere it's up to the hospital. I'll get you to the gates. You're beat up enough they'll take you.

AMELIA. You can't. You haul me to those gates and those raiders will get you for sure. You gotta hide.

KETCHAM. No, ma'am. You couldn't get there on your own. I betrayed "Miller." I'll be damned if I betray Amelia.

(KETCHAM kneels down, tenderly helps AMELIA up.)

Thank you, ma'am. Let's go find, Ethan.

(KETCHAM puts AMELIA on his back with her arms around his neck. KETCHAM moves slowly across the stage.)

Keep an eye out for them raiders.

AMELIA. Ketcham!

(A strident sound signals a blow to KETCHAM's head. They both tumble.)

(A GUARD sets AMELIA on a stretcher and then stands upright, his back to her as though carrying the cot.)

The guards agree to take me out – bad as I look now. The gates are closing on that hellhole as I watch Ketcham stumble back to the waiting raiders.

(GUARD sets her down, gets her off the cot, gathers cot, and starts to leave.)

Where's the hospital?

GUARD. This is it, them couple a tents and any shade you can find. Doctor'll get to you when he does.

AMELIA. I need to find a soldier – one leg turned black.

GUARD. You must be crazy. There's over a thousand out here right now. Take a look around.

AMELIA. Talks about a girl a lot, maybe sings…

(The GUARD stops and turns.)

GUARD. One leg gone bad?

AMELIA. *(She nods.)* I got some money. You can have it all.

GUARD. Where?

AMELIA. My left boot.

> *(The GUARD looks in her boot.)*

GUARD. Two bucks? That's it! Shit.

> *(Takes the money and starts to leave.)*

AMELIA. Wait. I've got this!

> *(She shows silver cross around neck. He holds it in his hand, rubs it.)*

GUARD. Silver. Yeah, alright, I'll take it.

> *(Breaks necklace.)*

That boy ain't been talking or singing in a while. So, no guarantees. Hey! Give me a hand here!

> *(Shouts to another guard.)*

Over to that big pine tree.

> *(The GUARD comes back in carrying a prisoner over his shoulder.)*

Ain't much left. Looks dead to me.

> *(The GUARD flops the prisoner down next to AMELIA. GUARD leaves. Pause.)*

AMELIA. Is it you? I don't have the strength for it not to be.

> *(AMELIA finally looks at the slumped man next to her. She slowly reaches out and touches his face. She starts to weep.)*

ETHAN. *(Stirs.)* What's wrong, soldier? Miss your family?

AMELIA. Yes, sir.

ETHAN. Me too, boy. Me too. My Amelia is the most beautiful creature on earth. Think of her all the time.

AMELIA. I'm sure she thinks of you.

ETHAN. I hope so.

AMELIA. I know so.

ETHAN. You do?

AMELIA. Yes, Ethan.

> (**ETHAN** *adjusts his body, in a great deal of pain, to look at her, slowly realizing.*)

ETHAN. My sweet Amelia, what have you done?

> (**ETHAN** *shakily reaches out for her hand. They are quiet for a moment holding hands.*)

AMELIA. Feels good to hold your hand.

> (**ETHAN** *gently kisses her hand.*)

ETHAN. Long way to come to hold someone's hand.

AMELIA. It was worth it.

> (*He touches her bruised face.*)

ETHAN. What's happened to you?

AMELIA. Getting here took a bit of a toll.

ETHAN. *(Touches her hair.)* You cut your hair.

AMELIA. I was scared you wouldn't recognize me.

> (*Pause.*)

ETHAN. Amelia, I dream of you…talk about you, sing to you day and night but most of all…you walking into this place to find me… I recognize you, alright.

AMELIA. Ethan…we don't look so good.

ETHAN. I know. Kept wondering why I was hanging on so long.

> (**AMELIA** *reaches over with pain, difficulty and attempts a hug with one arm.*)

AMELIA. Mama said to give you a hug when I seen you.

> (*Silence.*)

Mama and Daddy are sure gonna be glad to see us.

> (**ETHAN** *looks at her for a long moment and then decides to join in.*)

ETHAN. Yeah.

> (*Pause.*)

ETHAN. First thing I'll do when I seen that ol' gal is give her a bear hug and demand a double share of those apple pancakes of hers.

AMELIA. Mmmm, covered in cinnamon and fresh butter.

(He lays his head down.)

ETHAN. And then…

(She laughs a little and looks down at him and strokes his hair. They are now in the exact position that they were in at the beginning of the play.)

AMELIA. And then after we're full up Daddy'll get out his fiddle and start to play.

ETHAN. Don't ask me to dance.

*(**AMELIA** laughs.)*

AMELIA. Why not?

ETHAN. I think you know.

(She laughs again.)

AMELIA. Watching you dance that night at the ferry landing. So serious and proud. You were so bad!

(She laughs.)

ETHAN. Hey, come on now.

AMELIA. That's the bravest thing I've ever seen.

ETHAN. Brave? I don't know about that. How about you and that Brahma bull? Remember that?

AMELIA. Oh yeah.

ETHAN. Tell me that story.

AMELIA. Ethan, listen. Just before you left that night you told me you loved me and I –

ETHAN. It's alright –

(Grabs her hand, pain…recovers.)

The Brahma bull. Tell me that one.

AMELIA. Ethan…

ETHAN. *(Drifting in and out.)* Go on. Tell it. Please.

AMELIA. *(Pause.)* First thing Daddy would tell people, after showing 'em his black and purple scar running foot to kneecap – first thing he'd say, pointing over at me: "See that gal right there, little slip of a thing. Stared down a two thousand pound Brahma bull…"

> *(She trails off as she looks down at* **ETHAN** *– he is not moving. She pulls him in close, strokes his face and hair. She takes him in for a long moment and then begins to sing in a whisper.)*

"THE WATER IS WIDE, I CANNOT CROSS OVER, AND NEITHER HAVE I WINGS TO FLY. GIVE ME A BOAT THAT CAN CARRY TWO AND BOTH SHALL ROW, MY LOVE AND I…"

The End

www.ingramcontent.com/pod-product-compliance
Lightning Source LLC
Chambersburg PA
CBHW070357120726
47909CB00008B/2889